WITHDRAWN
ONTARIO CITY LIBRARY
W9-APS-233

Is someone after Cam and Eric?

Cam walked ahead. Then she stopped. She held out her hand and Eric stopped, too. She put her finger in front of her mouth so that he would be quiet. They listened. They heard the sounds of coins and keys jingling. Someone was walking behind them and was getting closer.

Jingle.

Jingle.

"What should we do?" Eric asked.

Cam looked across the backyard. It was surrounded by a metal fence.

Jingle.

Cam whispered, "Let's run around the back of the house to the other side and then out."

Jingle.

Cam and Eric started to run. Whoever was following them started to run, too.

"Stop! Stop running right now!" someone called out.

CAM JANSEN

CASE #14

The Chocolate Fudge Mystery

David A. Adler

Illustrated by Susanna Natti

PUFFIN BOOKS
An Imprint of Penguin Group (USA) Inc.

PUFFIN BOOKS
Published by the Penguin Group
Penguin Young Readers Group, 345 Hudson Street, New York, New York 10014, U.S.A.
Penguin Group (Canada), 90 Eglinton Avenue East, Suite 700, Toronto, Ontario, Canada M4P 2Y3
(a division of Pearson Penguin Canada Inc.)
Penguin Books Ltd, 80 Strand, London WC2R 0RL, England
Penguin Ireland, 25 St Stephen's Green, Dublin 2, Ireland (a division of Penguin Books Ltd)
Penguin Group (Australia), 250 Camberwell Road, Camberwell, Victoria 3124, Australia
(a division of Pearson Australia Group Pty Ltd)
Penguin Books India Pvt Ltd, 11 Community Centre,
Panchsheel Park, New Delhi - 110 017, India
Penguin Group (NZ), 67 Apollo Drive, Rosedale, North Shore 0632, New Zealand
(a division of Pearson New Zealand Ltd)
Penguin Books (South Africa) (Pty) Ltd, 24 Sturdee Avenue,
Rosebank, Johannesburg 2196, South Africa

Registered Offices: Penguin Books Ltd, 80 Strand, London WC2R 0RL, England

First published in the United States of America by Viking,
a division of Penguin Books USA Inc., 1993
Published by Puffin Books, a division of Penguin Books USA Inc., 1995, 1999
This edition published by Puffin Books, a division of Penguin Young Readers Group, 2011

21 23 25 27 29 30 28 26 24 22

THE LIBRARY OF CONGRESS HAS CATALOGED THE VIKING EDITION AS FOLLOWS:
Adler, David A.
Cam Jansen and the chocolate fudge mystery / David A. Adler ;
illustrated by Susanna Natti.
p. cm.—(Cam Jansen series; #14)
Summary: When Cam Jansen and her friend Eric uncover a mystery while
selling fudge door-to-door to raise money for the local library,
Cam uses her photographic memory to foil a crime.
ISBN: 0-670-84968-5 (hardcover)
[1. Mystery and detective stories.] I. Natti, Susanna, ill. II. Title.
III. Series: Adler, David A. Cam Jansen adventure; 14.
PZ7.A2615Caae 1993 [Fic]—dc20 93-18622 CIP AC

Puffin Books ISBN 978-0-14-240211-5

Printed in the United States of America

RL: 2.3

To my nephew Donnie,
who inspired my very first book,
and to his lovely bride, Aliza

Chapter One

Cam Jansen's father looked up. He was sitting in his car and reading a mystery novel. He was also waiting for Cam and her friend Eric Shelton. They were selling chocolate fudge bars and rice cakes to raise money for a local charity.

Mr. Jansen saw Eric look at a sheet of paper. *He's trying again,* Mr. Jansen thought. *I hope this time he can remember his speech.*

Eric Shelton put the paper in his pocket. Then he turned to Cam and said, "Good morning or afternoon. We're here to . . .

to . . . to . . . Oh, I can't remember what to say."

Cam said, "Let me try."

Cam put the shopping bag she was carrying on the sidewalk. She took a chocolate bar and a rice cake from the bag. Then she closed her eyes and said, "*Click.*"

Cam smiled. With her eyes still closed, she said, "Good afternoon. We're here to raise money for Ride and Read. We bring homebound elderly people to our local library. By buying this chocolate fudge bar or this rice cake, you will help us with our work."

Cam opened her eyes.

"You got every word right," Eric said. "I've been studying and studying that speech and I still can't remember it. How long did it take you to memorize it?"

"I looked at it once, blinked my eyes and said '*Click*' and I knew it."

Cam has what people call a photographic memory. She remembers just about every-

thing she sees. It's as if she has photographs stored in her brain. Cam says *"Click"* is the sound her mental camera makes when it takes a picture.

Cam's real name is Jennifer Jansen. When she was very young, people called her "Red" because she has red hair. But when they found out about her amazing memory, they began calling her "The Camera." Soon "The Camera" was shortened to "Cam."

Cam and Eric walked up the front path of a small brick house. There was a large broom next to the front door. Eric moved it aside and rang the doorbell. An old woman with curly white hair, wearing a long, frilly apron, came out.

"Good afternoon," Cam said. "We're here to raise money—"

"Good afternoon," the woman answered.

Cam started her speech again. "Good afternoon. We're here to raise money for Ride and Read."

"That's wonderful," the woman said. "Ride and Read is a fine program. Sometimes they take my husband to the library.

Now, don't say another word. I want my husband to meet you."

Then she called, "Jacob. Jacob!" Her husband, an old man with rosy cheeks and a bushy white mustache, came to the door.

The woman introduced her husband and herself to Cam and Eric. "This is Mr. Jacob Miller and I'm Mrs. Janet Miller."

"My name is Jennifer Jansen," Cam said, "and this is my friend, Eric Shelton."

The woman told her husband, "These children are raising money for Ride and Read."

"Good afternoon," Cam said. Then she waited. She expected to be interrupted again. When Mrs. Miller didn't say anything, Cam went on.

When Cam had finished her speech, Mr. Miller smiled. "What you're doing is nice, but I don't eat candy and I've never tasted a rice cake."

"What about me?" Mrs. Miller asked. "I love chocolate. And anyway, it's for charity. We'll take two of each."

Eric gave her the chocolate fudge bars and rice cakes. Mrs. Miller paid Eric. He put the money in an envelope.

As Cam and Eric went to the next house, Eric said, "That was easy."

A man and woman were running toward them. They were looking straight ahead and swinging their arms as they ran.

"Let me talk this time," Eric said. "I think I can remember what to say."

Eric took a chocolate bar and a rice cake from the shopping bag. When the runners were a few steps away, Eric smiled and said, "Good afternoon. We're here to raise money . . ."

The runners didn't stop.

"Hm," Eric said. Then he pointed to a woman who was walking along the side of the yellow house next door. She was wearing

a long blue raincoat and dark glasses. She was carrying a large, filled, black plastic bag. When she reached the sidewalk, she turned and walked quickly toward Cam and Eric.

"Good afternoon," Eric said. "We're here to raise money . . ."

The woman didn't look at Eric. She just kept on walking.

"Hm," Eric said again.

Cam looked straight at the woman. Just as she was about to walk past, Cam blinked her eyes and said, *"Click."*

"Those people were rude," Eric said. "Didn't they know I was talking to them?"

Cam kept watching the woman. Then she whispered to Eric, "That woman is hiding something. She's wearing dark glasses and it isn't sunny out. She's wearing a raincoat and it's not raining. There's something in that bag that shouldn't be there. Let's follow her."

Chapter Two

"You can't just follow people," Eric said. "There must be some law against doing that. And anyway, we came here to sell candy, not to play detective."

"I'm not playing. I *am* a detective and you know it. I've already caught a few criminals. You helped me. Now are you coming with me or not?"

Cam started to follow the woman. Eric grabbed the shopping bag and joined her.

Crinkle! Crinkle!

"Shh," Cam said.

Crinkle! Crinkle!

"Shh!" she said again.

Eric whispered, "I can't help it. It's the rice cakes. They make noise when they move around in the bag."

Brooom! Brooom!

A gardener was mowing a lawn across the street.

Cam and Eric saw the woman stop in front of a blue house, right next to two garbage cans. She looked quickly to the right and then to the left. Then she lifted the lid of a garbage can and dropped the plastic bag in.

Cam and Eric watched as she crossed the street. She walked quickly past the gardener and into a large white house.

When the door closed, Cam said, "Let's see what's in that bag."

"We have no right to look in there. It's not our garbage," Eric told her.

"It's garbage," Cam said. "She threw it away. Now it belongs to anyone who wants

it. There might be evidence of some terrible crime in there. That's why she crossed the street to throw it away. Maybe she robbed a bank and the bag is filled with those small paper bands they put around the money."

"And maybe the woman had a party last night," Eric said. "She's wearing dark glasses because her eyes hurt. She's wearing a long coat because underneath it, she has on a nightgown. This morning, she was too tired to get completely dressed. And there was so much trash from her party that she couldn't fit it all in her own garbage can."

When Eric finished talking he smiled and folded his arms.

"Maybe you're right," Cam said. "Let's find out."

Cam walked ahead and Eric followed her. They had reached the blue house. Cam was about to lift the lid of the garbage can.

"Stop!" Eric said. "Don't lift that lid."

"Why not?"

"It's not your garbage," Eric said.

"Oh, that's silly."

Cam began to lift the lid again.

"Stop!" Eric told her. "There may be a bomb in there."

Chapter Three

Cam very gently put the lid down.

Eric said, "You know, we were told in safety class not to go near strange packages."

Cam stepped away from the garbage can. She closed her eyes and said, "*Click.*"

"What are you trying to remember?" Eric asked.

Cam "*clicked*" again. Then she said, "I was looking at the pictures I had in my head of that woman carrying the bag. She wasn't holding it like she was afraid it would explode. And she just dropped it in the garbage can. She wouldn't have done that if there was a bomb inside."

Cam lifted the lid again. She opened the bag and looked inside.

"What do you see? What's in there?" Eric asked.

"Lots of apple peels."

Cam shook the bag.

"There's an empty skim milk carton under the peels and an empty box of oat bran," Cam said.

Eric leaned closer.

"Yuck," he said. "It stinks."

Then he looked in and said, "Maybe the paper money bands are at the bottom."

Cam rolled up her sleeves and dug into the bag.

"What's in there?" Eric asked.

"More garbage."

Cam pulled out a few soda cans, some paper plates, an orange juice carton, and a cereal box.

ELSIE-O
SKIM MILK
OAT BRAN
super healthy!
JUICE

"Super Sweet Wheats!" Eric said. "And the box top is still attached."

He tore the top off the cereal box. "I can send this in and get a Super Sweet Wheats watch," he said. He put the box top in his pocket.

Cam shook the bag again. She reached in and took out a large envelope. It was empty.

"Nothing but garbage," she said. Then she put it all back in the bag.

Cam put the lid on the can. She was about to roll down her sleeves, when she smelled her hands.

"Yuck! Now my hands stink! If I roll down my sleeves, my shirt will stink, too."

Cam stretched her hands out. She told Eric she was keeping her smelly hands away from the rest of her. Then Cam said, "I just don't understand it. That woman looked so guilty and mysterious."

"Oh, everything is a mystery to you," Eric said as they walked past the Miller house.

Eric kicked two rolled up newspapers out of the way as he and Cam walked up the front path of the yellow house next door.

Eric rang the front doorbell. He waited. Then he rang it again. He knocked on the door, but there was no answer.

"There's probably no one at home," he said.

Cam nodded. "Look at these newspapers. It looks like no one has been here for a while."

They each picked one up and looked at it. Eric read the headline, "Ding, Dong! Four-Alarm Fire Blazes On."

"Mine says that, too," Cam said. "These newspapers are from last week."

She dropped the paper and walked toward the back of the house. Eric ran after her and asked, "What are you doing now?"

"I still think that woman with the dark glasses was up to something and I want to find out what it was. We first saw her walking along the side of this house. Maybe there's a shortcut back here or maybe some secret hideaway."

"Oh, stop talking about that woman," Eric said, but he followed Cam.

All the windows of the yellow house were closed and the shades were down. Cam lifted the lids of the two garbage cans that were along the side of the house. Both were empty.

Cam walked ahead. Then she stopped. She held out her hand and Eric stopped, too. She put her finger in front of her mouth so that he would be quiet. They listened.

They heard the sounds of coins and keys jingling. Someone was walking behind them and was getting closer.

Jingle.

Jingle.

"What should we do?" Eric asked.

Cam looked across the backyard. It was surrounded by a metal fence.

Jingle.

Cam whispered, "Let's run around the back of the house to the other side and then out."

Jingle.

Cam and Eric started to run. Whoever was following them started to run, too.

"Stop! Stop running right now!" someone called out.

Chapter Four

Cam and Eric stopped running. Cam held Eric's hand and they slowly turned around.

"What are you doing here? I told you that I had to be able to see you from my car at all times."

It was Cam's father.

"You're standing on someone's private property," he said. "You're not supposed to be here."

"Did you see that woman with the dark glasses?" Cam asked. "She looked mysterious to me. She was walking back here. I just wanted to find out what she was up to. She may have been involved in a crime."

Mr. Jansen was holding a book. He showed it to Cam. "Do you see this? If you want to solve crimes, do what I do. Read a mystery. It's safer. Now let's get out of here."

Tinkle.

Tinkle.

Someone or something was moving nearby.

"Watch out!" Eric called.

He jumped to get out of the way of a black-and-white cat. A small bell was tied around its neck. The cat leaped onto the back porch and poked its head into a cardboard box.

"Let's go," Cam's father said.

The cat pulled on the box and tipped it over. Containers of milk and juice, a box of Super Sweet Wheats, and a wrapped loaf of bread fell out. The cat bit into the plastic wrapping around the bread. It ran with the

loaf to the far end of the yard, right in front of the metal fence.

Mr. Jansen started to walk toward the front of the house. He called to Cam and Eric, "I expect both of you to be following me."

Cam caught up with her father and asked him, "If there's no one at home, why is there food on the back porch?"

"Maybe there's a homebound person

living in that house, someone too sick to go shopping," he answered, "and he has his groceries delivered."

"And too sick to come to the door to buy chocolate or rice cakes," Eric added.

Cam, Eric, and Cam's father had walked to the front sidewalk. Mr. Jansen stopped.

"Something stinks," he said. He checked the bottoms of his shoes.

"It's my hands," Cam said. "I was looking through some garbage."

"What!"

Just then a letter carrier turned the corner.

"Make sure you wash your hands," Mr. Jansen told Cam.

Mr. Jansen looked at the letter carrier walking toward them. Then he said, "There's a mailbox next to the front door and it's empty. Either someone is in this house and is taking in the mail, or the people who live here are on vacation and have stopped their mail delivery. We'll see in a minute."

The letter carrier went up the Millers' front walk. He put some letters and a magazine in their box. Then he walked toward the yellow house.

Mr. Jansen smiled.

"Good afternoon," the letter carrier said, as he walked past.

He didn't deliver anything to the yellow house.

"Well, no one is home," Eric said. He picked up the bag of candy and rice cakes. "Now let's raise some money for Ride and Read."

Cam stared at the yellow house. "You say no one is home, but there's a box of food on the back porch."

Cam looked at the front windows and at the closed curtains hanging inside. She looked at the outdoor furniture that was

neatly stacked on the front porch, and the many newspapers on the front lawn.

Cam "*clicked.*"

She "*clicked*" again.

Cam stared at the house for another minute. Then she said slowly, "Someone went to a lot of trouble to make us think that no one is living in this house. But that woman probably brought that box of food here and the garbage she was carrying was from this house. There is someone hiding in there and I'm going to find out who it is."

Chapter Five

Cam quickly went next door. She found a spot in the Millers' yard where she could see between the hedge and the fence. She sat on the grass and watched the back of the yellow house.

"Why is she so sure that someone is hiding here?" Mr. Jansen asked Eric.

Eric shrugged his shoulders and shook his head. He didn't know.

"And where did she go?"

Eric shook his head again.

Eric and Mr. Jansen walked ahead,

toward the Millers' house. Then Mr. Jansen saw Cam sitting in the Millers' backyard.

"She can't do that. She shouldn't be sitting on someone else's lawn," Mr. Jansen said.

"We know the people who live here," Eric said. "They bought candy and rice cakes from us. We can ask them if Cam can stay there."

Mr. Jansen stood behind Eric as he rang the doorbell of the Millers' house. Mrs. Miller came out wearing the same long, frilly apron.

"Hello again," she said. "The chocolate fudge bar is delicious."

"The rice cakes are good, too," Eric said.

Mr. Jansen stepped forward.

"My daughter is Jennifer Jansen, the pretty girl with red hair and freckles who came to your house earlier. She's sitting in your yard right now and watching the yellow house next door. If you don't want her there, I'll tell her to leave."

"She thinks someone is hiding in there," Eric added.

"She does? Oh, my goodness! I must tell Jacob."

Mrs. Miller came back a moment later with her husband.

"The Pells live next door," Mr. Miller said, "but they're on vacation. They won't be back for several weeks."

"Someone left a box of food on the back porch," Eric said. "Cam is watching to see if anyone will come out and get it."

"Who is Cam?" Mrs. Miller asked.

"Jennifer's nickname is Cam," Mr. Jansen explained. "It's short for 'The Camera.' We call her that because she has a photographic memory."

"Oh, well, your camera daughter might be right," Mrs. Miller said. "The Pells' nephew may be in the house. I've never met him, but I know he's a writer. Mrs. Pell has told me that he has trouble finding a quiet place to work."

"Let's go outside and see if Jennifer has seen anyone," Mr. Miller said.

Mr. Jansen and Eric waited while Mrs. Miller took off her apron and hung it in the closet. She put on a straw hat with a wide brim.

They all walked to the backyard. Eric sat on the grass next to Cam. The Millers and Mr. Jansen stood next to them.

Mr. Jansen asked Cam, "What makes you so sure there's someone hiding in there?"

"It's the newspapers on the front lawn," Cam said.

"The newspapers!" her father said. "That's a sure sign that no one is in the house."

"I smell something," Mrs. Miller said.

"Shh," Eric said. "I hear something."

Mr. Jansen and the Millers bent down, so they were hidden by the hedges.

They were quiet. They didn't see anyone, but they heard something or someone moving.

Tinkle.

Meow!

The black-and-white cat jumped onto the back porch again. With its paws and mouth, it tried to open the cardboard carton of milk.

Mr. Jansen and the Millers stood up.

"Eric and I each looked at a newspaper," Cam said, "and both papers had the same headline. Whoever is hiding in that house probably bought a bunch of papers the day he went into hiding, rolled them up, and threw them on the lawn so people would think the house was empty."

Eric said, "The woman with the dark glasses may have thrown the papers there."

The cat pulled the milk carton to the edge of the steps and stepped away. The carton fell down the steps and tore open. The cat began to lick up the spilled milk.

Suddenly the cat stopped. It looked up. Its legs were bent. The cat was ready to run.

"It heard something," Mr. Jansen whispered.

He and the Millers bent down.

There was a creaking sound. Then the back door of the yellow house opened.

Chapter Six

"Scram!"

A tall, thin man with a light brown beard came out of the house. He was wearing blue jeans and a dark green shirt. The man ran across the back porch and chased the cat away.

Cam stood up. She looked straight at the man, blinked her eyes and said *"Click."* Then she quickly sat down.

The man watched the cat run off. He picked up the juice carton, cereal box, and the few other groceries that were on the

porch. He put them all in the large box and carried them into the house.

"That's not Mr. Pell," Mr. Miller whispered.

"I'll bet he's a criminal and that house is his hideaway. We should call the police," Eric said.

"I can't keep standing here. I'm tired," Mrs. Miller said. "Let's go inside."

Eric and Mr. Jansen followed the Millers into the house. Cam continued to watch the back of the yellow house. The door opened. The tall, thin man came outside. He was carrying a broom and a large, empty, black plastic bag. He looked around. Then he walked down the steps of the back porch. He put the empty milk carton in the bag. Then he swept away as much of the milk as he could. The man turned and looked right at where Cam was sitting. He stood there for a minute. Then he went into the house.

Cam waited. When the man didn't come out again, she joined Eric and the others in the Millers' kitchen. Cam washed her hands with soap. Then she looked to see what the others were doing.

Cam's father and the Millers were sitting by the table drinking coffee and eating cookies, chocolate fudge bars, and rice cakes. Eric was reaching into a large paper bag filled with newspapers.

"The Millers recycle their newspapers," Eric told Cam, "and the pickup isn't until tomorrow. I'm looking for the paper with the *Ding, Dong* headline. If we find that, we'll know when the man went into hiding."

Mrs. Miller was eating a rice cake. She put it down and said, "I think he's the Pells' nephew. Mrs. Pell told me how hard he works and how he hates to be disturbed when he writes."

"Is her nephew tall and thin?" Cam asked. "Does he have a beard?"

"Maybe. I've never seen him."

Eric emptied the bag of newspapers onto the kitchen floor. The daily newspapers, a few supermarket flyers, and the weekly community newspaper fell out.

"Here it is. Here's the *Ding, Dong* paper," Eric said. "Now I'm going to look for a report of an escaped criminal who is hiding somewhere."

"What's the date on that paper?" Cam asked.

Eric showed her the masthead. "It's Tuesday's newspaper."

Cam looked through the pile of newspapers on the floor. She found the Wednesday newspaper and began to look through it.

Mr. Jansen put down his cup of coffee and asked Cam, "Why are you looking at Wednesday's paper?"

"If that man went into hiding on Tuesday for something he just did, then it would be written up in the next day's paper, on Wednesday," Cam explained.

When Eric heard that, he closed his newspaper. He looked through the Wednesday paper with Cam.

"Some stores will deliver groceries," Mrs. Miller said. "If the Pells' nephew is busy writing, he may not have time to go shopping.

That's why there was a box of food on the back porch."

Cam turned the page of the newspaper.

Mrs. Miller went on. "Many years ago, I tried to write a story for a mystery magazine, but as soon as I sat down to write, the telephone rang. Then the mail was delivered. Then it was time for me to eat lunch. The Pells' nephew probably just doesn't want to be disturbed. That's why he's pretending that no one is at home."

“Look at this,” Eric said. He pointed to a column with the headline, *Crime Watch.*

Eric picked up the newspaper and read from it.

“In a daring robbery today at the Midtown Savings Bank a teller was handed a withdrawal slip for $10,000. ‘You must fill in your account number and sign your name,’ the teller told the man. The man showed the teller a gun and said, ‘You have just one minute to give me the money.’ The thief is described as tall and thin, with light brown hair.”

“That’s him. That’s the man hiding next door,” Cam said.

Chapter Seven

Mr. Miller picked up the telephone. He pressed a few buttons, waited, and then said, "There's a bank thief hiding in the house next door and he has a gun." Then he gave the police the address of the yellow house.

Cam, Eric, Mr. Jansen, and the Millers went to the front window to watch for the police.

While the others looked to the right, toward the yellow house, Cam looked for a moment the other way. She saw a woman come out of the large white house across the street. She was carrying a suitcase.

"Look," Cam said. "It's that woman again. She's walking this way. Maybe her friend saw us watching him and now they're going to run away."

Cam ran to the front door of the Millers' house and went outside.

"Wait. The police will get her," Mr. Miller called.

Mr. Jansen said, "I have to stop her. That woman might be dangerous."

Mr. Jansen and Eric quickly followed Cam outside.

Cam was holding the broom, pretending to be sweeping the front walk. She was really watching to see what the woman would do.

"Stop!" Mr. Jansen called out.

Cam stopped sweeping. She turned to look at her father. The woman stopped, too.

"Now she knows that I'm watching her," Cam whispered.

The woman turned and began to run the other way.

Cam dropped the broom and ran to the sidewalk. She looked straight at the running woman, blinked her eyes and said, "*Click.*" Then she started to walk after the woman.

Screech!

Suddenly there were flashing lights as three police cars quickly turned the corner. They sped past the running woman and Cam. Mr. Jansen waved his hands and signaled them to stop. The first two didn't. They sped past Mr. Jansen to the front of the yellow house. But the third car stopped. There were two police officers sitting on the front seat.

Mr. Jansen spoke quickly through the open window of the car.

"My daughter. It's dangerous. She's following that woman." He was too upset to speak clearly.

Eric explained, "You just passed a woman who was running with a suitcase. She is a partner of the thief." Eric pointed to Mr. Jansen. "His daughter is following her."

"Get in," one of the police officers said.

Eric and Mr. Jansen sat in the back of the police car. The officer driving the car was a woman with short blond hair. The name on her tag was "Robinson."

The other officer was a man. The name on his tag was "Gomez." He turned to the back and told Eric and Mr. Jansen, "Put your seat belts on."

"My daughter has red hair," Mr. Jansen said.

"And the woman she's following has long brown hair," Eric told the police. "She's wearing dark glasses and a long blue raincoat."

Officer Robinson quickly turned the car around and sped toward Cam and the woman. Cam was in the middle of the next block. Officer Robinson stopped the car and Cam got in.

"The woman just went around the corner," Cam said. Then she told her father, "Don't worry, I wasn't getting too close."

They turned the corner. Officer Robinson drove slowly down the street, and they all looked for the woman.

There were many people going in and out of stores along the street. Then, at the end of the block, they saw the woman run into a large supermarket. Officer Robinson stopped the car. She and Officer Gomez ran out, past some people pushing shopping carts, and into the store. Cam, Eric, and Mr. Jansen were right behind them.

There were many aisles lined with shelves of cans, boxes, and bags of food. And there were many people pushing shopping carts and a few lines of people waiting to pay for their groceries.

“You wait here so she can’t get out,” Officer Robinson said to her partner. “I’ll search the store.”

Cam, Eric, and Mr. Jansen went with Officer Robinson. They walked through the entire store, but they didn’t find the woman.

“Is there another way out of here?” Officer Robinson asked one of the people who worked in the store.

"There's an emergency exit by the frozen food cases," the worker answered, "but if you open the door, a loud bell sounds."

They walked to the emergency exit. The door was closed.

"Let's keep looking," Officer Robinson said. "It shouldn't be so difficult to find a woman here carrying a suitcase."

Then, just beyond the dairy case Eric stopped. "Look," he said and pointed to a suitcase, a blue raincoat, a wig of brown hair, and a pair of dark glasses lying on the floor. "She's not carrying a suitcase anymore. We'll never find her now."

Chapter Eight

"Oh, yes, we will. We'll find her," Cam said. Then she closed her eyes and *"clicked."*

"What is she doing?" Officer Robinson asked.

Mr. Jansen whispered, "She's trying to remember something."

Cam *"clicked"* again. Then she opened her eyes and said, "She was wearing a long raincoat, but it didn't reach all the way down. She has red sneakers on and blue jeans."

"Quick, grab those things," Officer

Robinson told Mr. Jansen. "We have to catch her before she leaves here."

When they got to the front of the store, they found Officer Gomez still standing there. "No one wearing a long coat and carrying a suitcase left while I was watching," he told his partner.

"Did anyone leave wearing red sneakers and blue jeans?" she asked.

He thought for a moment. Then he shook his head slowly and said, "I don't know. I wasn't looking at their feet."

The two police officers ran to the door and looked outside. Mr. Jansen followed them. Meanwhile, Cam walked slowly and quietly toward the people waiting to pay for their groceries.

"Where are you going?" Eric asked.

"Shh."

Cam pointed to the last line. Someone wearing red sneakers and blue jeans was crouched down, hiding behind the other shoppers.

Cam got closer. Then she looked at the front door and saw Officer Gomez standing there. He was about to come inside.

Cam jumped behind the woman and shouted, "Here she is! Don't let her run outside!"

When the woman heard that, she ran straight for the door, just as Cam had hoped

3
MEAT
2
1
RECYCLING CENTER

she would. She ran right into the arms of Officer Gomez.

"I'm innocent! I'm innocent!" the woman said. "I didn't rob the bank. Sam did. I just helped him hide."

Officer Gomez spoke softly. "Helping a criminal escape is a crime, too."

He took a printed card from his pocket. He read from it, warning the woman that anything she said could be used as evidence against her. He locked her in handcuffs and led her to the police car. Officer Robinson put the suitcase, coat, and wig in the trunk.

Both police officers thanked Cam, Eric, and Mr. Jansen for their help.

"It's lucky that you remembered she was wearing red sneakers," Officer Robinson said.

"That wasn't luck," Eric told her. "Cam always remembers whatever she sees."

The officers said they were sorry for driving off without Cam, Eric, and Mr. Jansen.

But with the woman sitting in the backseat, there was no room for them.

After the police officers left, Mr. Jansen said, "Well, we can't stay here. Let's walk back to my car."

They passed many shoppers along the way. Eric was anxious to sell them chocolate fudge bars and rice cakes for Ride and Read, but Cam didn't let him. She was in a hurry to see if the police had arrested Sam, the bank robber.

When they reached Mr. Jansen's car, they saw a few police cars parked in front of the yellow house.

"We'll watch from here," Mr. Jansen said. "The police don't need our help and it might be dangerous to get too close."

They saw the man who had been hiding in the yellow house come outside with his hands raised. He was followed by two police officers. The man was locked in handcuffs and led to a police car. Then, one after another, the police cars turned around and drove off.

The last police car stopped by Cam, Eric, and Mr. Jansen. A tall officer with gold braid on the shoulder of his jacket got out of the car. He came over to Mr. Jansen and introduced himself.

"I'm Captain Gardner. Are you the one who found the thief?"

Mr. Jansen shook his head and said, "No. It was my daughter, Jennifer, and her friend Eric."

"Well," Captain Gardner said as he shook Cam's hand and then Eric's hand. "On behalf of the people of this city, I thank both of you. I'm sure the local newspaper and TV reporters will want to know that two young children helped us find a dangerous criminal."

Captain Gardner took out a small notepad. He wrote Cam's and Eric's names and addresses.

"Now," Captain Gardner said, as he turned and started to walk to his car, "you've helped me. If at any time, I can help you, please let me know."

"Wait!" Eric called out. "You can help me now. We're selling chocolate fudge bars and rice cakes to raise money for Ride and Read. We bring homebound elderly to our local library."

Captain Gardner bought two rice cakes from Cam and Eric and told them, "Now follow me and I'll help you raise a lot more money for Ride and Read."

At the police station, Captain Gardner announced that Cam and Eric were raising money for charity. Many of the officers were eating lunch. Eric sold them chocolate bars and rice cakes for dessert. Cam entertained the police officers by doing memory tricks.

Cam looked at all the officers gathered around Eric. She closed her eyes and said, "*Click.*"

"Officer Adams has red hair," Cam said, "and his necktie is crooked. Officer Lopez has three rings on his left hand."

"Maybe she's peeking," one of the officers said. "Maybe her eyes are not closed all the way."

Cam turned around and went on.

"Officer Davis has a drop of mustard on her collar."

"She's amazing," Officer Davis said.

Mr. Jansen smiled and said, "Yes, she is. And she's *my* daughter!"